I Got Bank!

I GOT BANK!

What My Granddad Taught Me About Money

WRITTEN BY TERI WILLIAMS

ILLUSTRATIONS BY ACESGRAPHICS MIZORAM

THE Beckham
PUBLICATIONS GROUP, INC.
Silver Spring

I GOT BANK!
What My Granddad Taught Me About Money
Written by Teri Williams
Illustrations by Acesgraphics Mizoram

Published in the United States by
Beckham Publications Group, Inc.

Printed in China

ISBN: 978-0-9827943-7-1

Library of Congress Control Number: 2010938533

TABLE OF CONTENTS

I dedicate this book to my wonderful family—Kevin Cohee, Erin Cohee and Kevin Cohee Jr.—for supporting my passion to give back to urban communities. You're the best!

Thanks to my dad, Frank Williams, who along with my mom, the late Mattie L. Williams, taught me to be financially responsible.

There are so many people who have helped me grow from living in "the projects" and the rural South to gaining the wisdom to write this book. Thank you all.

I hope that I Got Bank! *helps children. I want you to become more financially aware and passionate. I believe passion and financial knowledge will provide a strong foundation for your success and happiness.*

I also hope that others who are inspired to teach financial literacy in new and more innovative ways will better reflect our urban communities and connect with our children. There is a great deal of brilliant work to be done in this area.

Finally, I thank the OneUnited Bank team, including all former and current board members and employees, for your wisdom, hard work and commitment to our mission.

Thanks to Beckham Publications Group and Barry Beckham. Your feedback has been invaluable in turning my vision into reality and improving my book.

I shall donate a percentage of sales income from the book to programs that support financial literacy for youth.

PART 1
MY SUMMER PLANS

CHAPTER 1

I'M ONLY TEN

I usually don't wake up this early on Saturdays. But for some reason, I couldn't sleep. I guess I shouldn't say for some reason, since I know the reason. Money!

Glad my mom, older brother and sister are still sleeping so I don't have to talk to anybody. Don't know why people feel a need to talk all the time or ask a bunch of questions. I'm always thinking TMT—too much talking.

Anyway, I make my way down the hall past everybody's rooms to the kitchen. The sun is blazing through the kitchen window. I can barely see the apartments across the street. But I can still hear the cars rolling past my house.

I see my bank statement from Community Unity Bank as I flip through a pile of mail on the kitchen table. The white envelope stands out. I sit down, open it quickly and glance at my name and account number.

I Got Bank!

Jazz Ellington
1001883683-1

But I really focus on my account balance, the amount of money in my bank account. It says two thousand-fifty dollars and twenty-three cents! Bling! I think my granddad would say, "Not bad for a 10-year-old."

A few years ago when I was six, after my granddad set up my account, I was so proud to have a few hundred bucks. Now that I got more, I'm just trying to hold on to it. Everybody in my family—my mom, Jackson and Jasmine—are trying to spend *my* money. I know it's not cool to just say no. How do you say no to your mom? But how do you save, when everybody wants to spend? I'm beginning to understand why my granddad used to say I'm an "old soul." At ten, I already feel like an old man in a young man's body.

Hmmm. I think I just heard Jackson moving around in his room across the hall. I better hide my bank statement. But not before I eat. I'm starved. Here's some cereal, but no milk. Dang! Maybe my mom will cook breakfast when she wakes up.

I might as well go back to bed. I creep past Jackson's and Jasmine's rooms. No sounds from my mom's bedroom across the hall from mine. It's still quiet. Guess I won't be eating for a while. I hide my bank statement with all the others in the back of my closet under some clothes. Then climb to the top bunk, pull the covers over my head to block out the light—and my crazy family—and try to go back to sleep.

CHAPTER 2

I GOT BANK

Later, my best friend Marquis walks in as usual without ringing the bell. He catches me by surprise. I'm sitting at the kitchen table and looking at a few bank statements and eating a bowl of dry cereal.

"Hey Jazz. What's this?" he asks grabbing one of my statements, while I try to hide the others. "You have a bank account?"

At first I start to say no, but then I feel "dissed". Why is he acting so surprised? "Man, I got bank," I said and throw another bank statement at him.

"Say what?" Marquis shouts as I see him notice my account balance. "How did you get all this money?"

I swing back, tip my chair and put my feet on the table, hoping my mom doesn't walk in. "Yeah its sweet, isn't it? It's because of my granddad. He told me when I was real young that if I want to be successful I got to have bank. And the sooner I learn the better off I'll be."

I Got Bank!

"So be *my* granddad! Teach me," Marquis says as he sits down at the table. I put my feet down, lean forward and look at my best friend the same serious way my granddad looked at me.

"Well, Key, he said it's real simple." I've been calling Marquis "Key" for as long as I can remember. "Just get an allowance the same as your age and save it all."

Marquis looks confused. "An allowance the same as your age?"

"Yeah. So my granddad set me up, so my allowance goes in my bank account at Community Unity Bank automatically. When I was five, I got five dollars a week. When I was six, I got six a week. Now I'm getting ten a week and I've already saved over two thousand dollars. By the time I'm eighteen, I'll have over fifteen thousand dollars."

Marquis jumps up and shouts, "For real? It's that simple?" I sit up and put my finger to my mouth for him to be quiet. I don't want anybody to hear us. I look through the kitchen doorway into the living room to see if anybody is listening. Nobody is there.

"Yeah, it's that simple. But he left out the hard part," I whisper. "The hard part is you have to stop people from spending your money. It's tough to save when everybody around you needs money. And saving it all, Key, means saving every dime and keeping your money safe from users—because they're everywhere!" I then take back my statements and lead Marquis down the hall to my room to play video games. For a minute, I'm feeling pretty good about money again. Sharing my secret with my best friend gave me a real boost.

CHAPTER 3

MY FAMILY

"Hey Jazz," Marquis yells the next day as he runs through my kitchen door with a soccer ball under his arms. "Let's go to the park." I look up quickly to find him towering over me. I think he grew an inch overnight. Still in my Sunday clothes, I'm standing over a trash can with a pair of scissors. "Alright," I say. "Right after I shred my bank statements." Marquis laughs. "Jazz, don't you think you're taking your bank account a bit too seriously?"

"Man, I need to watch my money." I say, snipping away. Last night I had a real incident. I found Jackson in my closet. Said he was looking for an old T-shirt. I threw him out, but I realized I can't hide my bank statements in my room anymore. I sat in Sunday school this morning, praying so hard to get home before Jackson woke up that I missed the whole lesson.

"I'm shredding my bank statements so nobody will get any ideas about using my money. I've taken out a lot of trash and cleaned a lot of rooms to earn it. And man, you'd be surprised how many folks want to spend it."

"Like who?" Marquis asks as he sits down at the kitchen table. I stop snipping and look at him as I try to explain.

"Well, just the other day my mom asked me for a loan because her car broke down. I mean, I was sweating bricks. I guess my allowance is taken out of her paycheck. So she told me, if I didn't give her a loan she was going to lose her job and stop paying my allowance."

"What? Are you serious?" Marquis asks. "I can't imagine my mom or dad asking me for money."

"Yeah and last week, Jasmine asked me for a hundred and fifty dollars so she could go to a concert! Can you believe a hundred and fifty dollars for a concert? Said if I loaned her the money, I would be the best little brother that ever lived and she would do my errands for a year!"

"Ah man, maybe you should give her the loan," Marquis says back. "I wish I had a sister to do my errands."

"No way, Key," I said as I start snipping again. "My granddad told me, "To be successful, get a weekly allowance and save it all." Did you hear *loan* in those words?"

"No."

"Exactly! So, I've been saving every dime. But I don't want anybody to know how much money I have." Suddenly, I notice something and stop snipping. "Hmmm, I'm going to keep this last statement so I can have a word with the bank. I think they're ripping me off."

CHAPTER 4

AM I BEING RIPPED OFF?

After school the next day, I walk the twenty blocks to the bank. I pass the barbershop where my mom used to take me. I feel the hair on my head. Feels like I need a cut. I pass the Chinese restaurant where my sister always orders shrimp fried rice. The sweet smell of Chinese food is making me hungry. I haven't eaten since lunch. Then I pass some stores and restaurants that I've never seen before. I'm definitely no longer in the 'hood. If I wasn't trying to get my money straight, I probably would've turned around. I finally walk up the wide steps to Community Unity Bank.

"May I help you", is the first thing I hear when I walk in. I look at the woman seated behind a big desk. She looks like my mom dressed in a business suit.

"Not sure," I say. "I'm here to see about my bank account."

"My name is Miss Benjamin," she says. "May I have your name and account number?" she asks, then turns to her computer.

Am I Being Ripped Off?

"My name is Jazz Ellington and here's my last bank statement. It has my account number, my balance of two thousand-fifty dollars and twenty-three cents and my interest rate of one percent." I put my bank statement on the desk.

"Yes it does. My, my, you have a nice size bank account for such a young man." She looks at the bank statement then looks back at me. "I see you live on thirty-fifth and Grandview. That's my old neighborhood. I grew up on Blue Hill Avenue. My parents still live on MLK Boulevard." Not sure why she felt the need to share this information. TMT. Too much talking! "Is your mother or father with you?" she asks as she looks all around me. I shake my head. "So how can I help you?" she asks.

"Well, I've been watching the news and they say rates have been going up. I also saw in the paper last week that Great National Bank is paying three percent and you're only paying me one percent. Are you guys ripping me off?"

The woman looks like she is about to laugh, but stops herself. "No, young man, we're not ripping you off. You see, you have a youth account which we offer to help young people save. It looks like you've been saving for a long time."

"Yeah, since I was five. My granddad told me, "To be successful, get an allowance the same as your age and save it all". And that's what I've been doing."

"Well your grandfather is very smart and taught you well. It looks like he set up your account well too. Most kids don't have bank accounts and don't understand the importance of saving. But it's never too late to learn."

"Yeah, you sound like my granddad. But are you going to get to the ripping off part soon?" I think she's stalling. And even though she looks like my mom, I'm not sure I like her. It's starting to feel strange in here. The building feels like a fortress with big doors and gates. She's sitting right by the door, but against the wall across from her is a row of people standing behind thick bullet-proof glass. It's like they're saying, we got all the money and you can't have none. I'm starting to feel out of place but I'm not going to show it. I know how to look tougher than I feel. Do it all the time in school.

"Yes, I'm sorry," she says. "You see, banks offer many kinds of accounts for different customers with different needs. We pay

I Got Bank!

interest—which is a percentage rate on your account balance. We want you to keep, or deposit, your money with us. So a one percent interest rate means that for every hundred dollars you have in the bank, we will pay you one dollar per year. We offer different rates for different bank accounts. As an example, we offer three percent on a certificate of deposit."

"A certificate of what?" I ask. "Are you saying I have to pass a test to get three percent?" Now I'm sure I don't like this woman.

"No, no, no! Not *that* kind of certificate. A certificate of deposit—or CD—is a bank account that lets you keep the same interest rate for an amount of time—like six months or one year—if you agree to keep your money in the bank for that time. Banks are willing to pay a higher interest rate for a longer amount of time, which we call a term. So, if you take some of your savings from your youth account and move it to a CD, you can earn a higher rate—like three percent—for a one year term."

"I get it. I can open a different account and get a higher rate. Great!" I say. "So since I plan on saving until I'm eighteen and in college, I'll take the eight-year CD for twenty-four percent!"

This time the woman does laugh. "Wait, we don't offer an eight-year CD or a twenty-four percent rate. But if you bring in your mother or father, we can talk about opening the best CD we have for you."

"Cool. You can talk to my mom about a car loan too, so she can get off my back!" I say. I might like this banker after all. I'm so excited I run the twenty blocks back home, thinking maybe she can solve the rest of my family's money problems too.

CHAPTER 5

I'M LEARNING THE SCORE

A few days later, Marquis walks into my room. He has a way of walking around my house like he lives here. Most times it's alright. But sometimes it's not. Like now.

My granddad bought this house as a rooming house, where he rented rooms to tenants. When you walk in the front door, you're in the living room in the middle of the house. On the right side, behind a swing door, is a big kitchen that was used by all the tenants. On the left side is a room that is now my mom's bedroom. These three front rooms face some apartment buildings, the Wingate projects, across the street. There's a long hall behind these rooms that goes through the house. On the other side of the hall are three other rooms that face the driveway in the back. One is across from the kitchen, which is now Jackson's room. Another is in the middle across from the living room, that's Jasmine's room. And a third is across from my mom's bedroom, which is mine. There's one bathroom at the end of the hallway, next to the kitchen. It's pretty big with two showers, an old bathtub and a toilet. Like the kitchen and living room, it was shared by all the tenants too.

My friends who live in Wingate think it's great that we have a house and I have my own room. But I always feel like a tenant waiting for somebody to come collect rent. When we lived across town, I used to come here with my granddad when he collected rent.

My room has blue walls, a tall dresser, an old desk and my bunk bed against the wall. From the window, I can see the driveway. Under the window are my video game player, an old TV and some books.

I'm sitting at my desk, taking a break when Marquis walks in.

"Hey Jazz, why are you sitting in the dark?" he asks.

"Because I feel like it. Why are you here, Marquis?"

"Because you told me to come over to study for our math test next week. Remember?" Marquis turns on the light.

"Oh, right. I knew that." I get up and squint to get used to the light. I ball up a piece of paper and toss it towards the trash. I miss. "I guess I'm just trying to get over my trip to the bank with my mom."

Marquis grabs the ball of paper, fakes a few moves and dunks it in the trash. "Right, you said you were going to triple your money for the next eight years...and maybe become a millionaire. Man, can I be your bodyguard?"

"My what?" I groan. "No, Key, you're so off track. Man, I'm not sure I can begin to explain it to you."

Marquis looks surprised. "Come on. Try me," he says.

I take the ball of paper out of the trash and toss it again. I miss again. "Okay," I say. "First of all, I moved my money to a CD, so now I earn three percent instead of one percent. So my interest rate tripled."

Marquis kicks the ball of paper with his right foot. It lands in the trash and he raises both hands for the goal. "That's what I said, triple your money! But how did you move your money to a CD? Did you record a demo or something?"

I Got Bank!

"No! Not a CD like a record. A certificate of deposit, which is a bank account that lets you keep the same rate for an amount of time—like a one year term—if you agree to keep your money in the bank for that time. It pays more than a youth savings account, which is what I had. So that's the good news." I take the ball out of the trash again and pitch it to Marquis.

"Okay. So what's the bad news?" Marquis bats the ball back to me but it hits me on the top of my head. I barely feel it.

"They wouldn't give my mom a car loan because she has a bad credit report," I mumble as I sit back down. I really don't feel like talking about it, but I know he's going to keep asking. Yep, TMT!

"A what? Is she going to jail?"

"No, not jail. But the bank won't lend her more money because she hasn't been making monthly payments on the money she already owes. Can you believe there are credit agencies that keep track of *who* you owe, *how much* you owe and whether you pay back your loans *on time*? And they give you a score. They said my mom's credit score is too low."

Marquis picks the ball up from the floor and squeezes it. "Oh, that is bad news. My mom said if I got a bad score, I would have to go to summer school." He looks at me and I can tell what he's thinking before he even says it. "Guess you're just going to have to lend her the money. Come on Jazz. You got bank!" He soft punches me on the arm.

He said exactly what I've been thinking. But I've also been thinking about my granddad. "Yeah, but my granddad said a loan is really a gift because you'll never get it back."

Marquis throws the ball in the trash. "What? You never told me that."

"Yeah, Key. It didn't make any sense to me, until now."

CHAPTER 6

SAVINGS POWER

All of a sudden, the days are long and hot. Summer is almost here and the school year is about over. After I miss a few days of school, I run into Marquis at the bus stop. He starts asking a bunch of questions about why I missed school. The fool told me he thought the bank had picked up my mom and took her to the pokey, leaving me to fend for myself. I told him I was just out because I had a bad cold.

"You okay?" Marquis asks. I nod, although I'm still tired. "I've been thinking about your mom and I got an idea!" Marquis continues. I'm not surprised. Marquis is always coming up with something. "Okay, shoot," I say.

"Well, we can hold a car wash next Saturday to make some money to get her car fixed. That way, you won't have to lend her money that you'll never get back!"

"Hmmm, sounds interesting," I say as I get on the bus. Marquis follows me and keeps talking. "We could make a big sign that says, "Car and Money Laundering—Only ten dollars."

I Got Bank!

I look back. "Money laundering?"

"Yeah, I heard that on the news last night," Marquis says. "Said a man was money laundering millions of dollars at Great National Bank. Ten dollars will seem cheap."

"Key, money laundering is not a good thing. It means that somebody is taking money from crimes like selling drugs and putting it in a bank to try to make it seem legit. They're taking their crime cash or dirty cash and trying to make it look like clean cash from a real business by putting it in the bank. People go to jail for that."

"For real? The man didn't look like a criminal. I mean, Jazz, he had on a suit and tie. He was carrying a brief case. He was even riding in a limo. I know you got bank and all, but I really don't think money laundering is a crime. Why would they call it laundry?"

I laugh because he's got a point. We find two seats in the back of the bus and I say, "Banks definitely come up with some strange names. They have CDs that don't have a thing to do with music. Branches that don't even have trees. And money laundering has nothing to do with washing. Sometimes I wonder if they came up with these names to keep kids in the dark. But it's really because banking is old school. So they use old school ways to describe things. Anyway, let's talk about the car wash."

"Okay. At ten dollars a wash, we could earn one hundred dollars on Saturday!"

"Great, but my mom needs one thousand dollars. It would take us ten Saturdays to earn that—basically all summer. My mom needs to get her car fixed now."

"Wow, you're right! But Jazz, you have over two thousand dollars in the bank and you never washed a car!"

"Yeah. My granddad told me I could never beat the power of saving a little each week. Man. was he right."

"Yeah, but, it seems like he should've told your mom. Or she should've listened!"

CHAPTER 7

MY BROTHER

"Jackson, no! I'm not opening a bank account with you. Are you crazy?" I start moving from room to room trying to get away from my older brother. But he follows me everywhere as I try to escape.

"Come on Jazz. If you co-sign, Community Unity Bank might let me open a checking account there."

"First of all, what's the big deal about a checking account, and why can't you open one on your own?" I ask. I'm now in my room, leaning on my desk and holding up my chair to make sure Jackson keeps his distance. He stands in the doorway.

"Jazz, I need a checking account to write checks and pay bills. I can also use the debit card that comes with it to pay for things at the store," he says while he's reading a text on his phone. Hearing him, I realize he didn't answer my main question.

"Okay, then why can't you open one on your own?" I ask.

I GOT BANK!

"Because I sort of messed up the one I had at Great National Bank," Jackson says, putting his phone in his pocket and leaning against the door.

As I look at my brother, I realize something. At eighteen years old, he looks like he just walked off a video shoot—tall, dark and very cool. His T-shirt looks like silk. His black belt has studs. His jeans have that worn, but expensive look. But looks can be deceiving. "What do you mean, you sort of messed up?" I ask.

"Well. Okay. I messed up. I didn't keep track of how much money I had in my account and I wrote too many checks. So some checks bounced," Jackson says. He sounds mad. Not at me, but at the checks.

"Bounced! How can paper bounce?" I ask.

"Not really bounce, like a ball. They call it bounce because if you give a store a check to pay for something and you don't have the money, the bank sends the check right back unpaid, which is why they call it a bounced check. Get it? Bounce back! So now the bank says I have a ChexSystems record. ChexSystems tells every bank that I had problems with my bank account. So now, no bank will give me a checking account. It's a long story, but I really learned from my mistakes," Jackson says.

Jackson is much older than me, but right now he's looking kind of short. Did I grow, or is he just smaller than I thought? "Okay. Then tell that to the bank," I call out.

Jackson comes in my room and sits down on my bed. His phone keeps buzzing in his pocket. "I did, but I don't think they believe me. But you're a good customer with no ChexSystems record. I'm sure they'll believe you."

At this point, I begin to understand. Jackson looks and sounds so smart, but acts so dumb. I stare at my brother. "Jackson, didn't Granddad talk to you too?"

"What? About saving my allowance and all that stuff?" Jackson asks as he reaches for his phone.

"Yeah, that. Am I the only person in this family that actually believed him?"

18

CHAPTER 8

I'm Upside Down

Jazz Ellington
June 20

Granddad, I wish you were here as I write to you. I really need your help. Yes…thanks to you…I got bank! But it's stressing me out! I mean, the "allowance the same as my age" idea was perfect. I guess you set it up so that mine comes automatically out of Mom's paycheck. She pays Jasmine and Jackson in cash every week. They thought I was the best kid brother for about a month. They get more than me, since they're older.

The "saving it all" was perfect too! So far, I've saved over two thousand dollars. By the time I'm eighteen, I'll have over fifteen thousand dollars! The problem is that I think I'm the only one who listened to you. No…I take that back. They all listened, but I'm the only one who believed you. And now they want my help. I'm the youngest, remember? It seems like now that I got bank, my life has turned upside down. Older folks, who are supposed to be helping me, are asking me for help. I'm trying to stay true to your words, but I want to help our family too. Did I miss a lesson?

CHAPTER 9

MY PLAN

Summer is here and school is finally almost over. I could smell and feel the heat burning the pavement as I walk home from the bus stop.

"Hey Jazz. You must have gotten an A on that math test," Marquis says as he catches up with me.

"Yeah I did, but why do you say that?" I ask.

"Because you're smiling and I haven't seen you smile in days." Marquis says.

I laugh because I know he's right. "Well, I met with my banker after school yesterday."

"Sweet," Marquis says. Since I showed him my bank account, I've been telling him about my family's money problems too. "Did the bank forget about your mom's low credit score? Or give Jackson a checking account? Or give Jasmine one hundred-fifty dollars for her concert tickets?" Marquis asks.

"No. No. And no," I respond. "But I told her everything and we came up with a plan. I'll need your help."

Marquis looks surprised. "Okay, shoot."

I sit on the stoop in front of my house and look across the street at Wingate apartments. "First, the bank can use my CD as collateral to loan my mom one thousand dollars to get her car fixed."

"Great, but what's collateral?"

"Collateral is something of value like a bank account or a house that can be used to repay a loan. If you take out a loan with collateral and you don't pay the loan back, the bank can take the collateral and sell it to get their money back. So, they're more willing to give you a loan if you have collateral. With my CD as collateral, the bank will give my mom the loan."

"Sweet! Now what about Jackson and Jasmine?" Marquis asks as he sits next to me and looks across the street.

"Well, my mom can open a checking account with Jackson, if Jackson takes a class called "How to Manage Your Checking Account." Even though my mom has a low credit score, she doesn't have a ChexSystems record, because she never bounced a check."

"Great again," Marquis says, "although I never heard of Chex-Systems and I didn't know that checks could bounce."

"Yeah, that's a long story. Anyway for Jasmine, she can earn the one hundred-fifty dollars for her concert tickets. That's where you come in. My banker loves your car wash idea!"

Marquis looks at me and smiles. "Really?"

"Yeah. In fact, she said that my whole family should join in to earn extra money on Saturdays. At fifty dollars a week, we could pay off my mom's loan, the money Jackson owes Great National Bank for his bounced checks and the one hundred-fifty dollars for Jasmine's concert tickets. It will take some time, but we could do it."

"Great! But I think we could earn one hundred dollars a week," Marquis says.

I take a notebook out of my backpack. "Yeah, but your family should get half. And my banker is ready to open a savings account for you too. She said if your mom agrees to my granddad's allowance plan, even though you're starting at ten years old instead of

I GOT BANK!

five, you'll still have over five thousand dollars when you're eighteen!" I open the notebook to the savings numbers that my banker wrote down for Marquis.

Marquis jumps up and starts dancing. "Yeah, Money. That's right. It's my birthday. It's my birthday!" Marquis takes the notebook and studies the page as he says to me, "So, your granddad was right. It pays to have bank!"

"Yeah, he was right on the money!"

PART 2
MAKING MONEY THIS FALL

CHAPTER 10

NEED TO FIND THE KEY

I pull the sheets down and lie on the top bunk looking at the ceiling. I don't feel like getting out of bed. I know I need to switch to the bottom bunk since I grew almost two inches over the summer. I'm way too big for a bunk bed. As I think about how much has changed this summer, I still feel like too much is the same.

The Saturday car wash is a big hit. We're making tons of money. I love working with my best friend, Marquis, and my mom and older brother and sister. We work as a team from sun up to sun down. Jasmine waves the cars off the street into our driveway. Jackson talks the drivers into taking a twenty-minute break to get their car hand-washed. Marquis and my mom do most of the washing. Soap and water splashes everywhere. That's big fun! I help out with the washing, collect the money and take care of any customer complaints—or customer suggestions as my mom calls them. It's been fun, but a lot of hard work. After ten straight Saturdays, I'm tired.

Even though the car wash is a success, I can tell we need more money. There's never enough food in the house. And when I compare all the nice cars we wash to my mom's car, her car looks like a train wreck...even after she got it fixed. Then there's the man from the city who says we need a license to run a car wash in our driveway. He's threatening to close us down. So I feel like we're running on a treadmill, going fast but staying in the same place. I look at the ceiling while thinking about finding the key to get to the other side—where there is money, success and happiness like I see on TV. I can't quite figure it out.

CHAPTER 11

WORKING AT THE CAR WASH

"Jazz, you got to get up," Marquis says as he runs in my room and tries to catch his breath. "Do you see how many people are lined up *again* to get their car washed? I mean every Saturday, they've been lining up. There are so many dirty cars around here. You should've seen the trash blowing in the wind on my way over here. It was a trash attack!"

I lift up to look out the window and see all the cars. "Man, I'm tired," I say as I flop back down. "Can you believe we've been washing twenty cars every Saturday? I hope we have enough money to pay back my mom's loan soon."

"Yeah and we can shut this car wash down before that man does. Plus, football practice starts next week." Marquis fakes throwing a football. "I'm tired of working every Saturday too."

I climb down from the top bunk. I'm already wearing some old gym shorts. I just need a shirt.

Working at the Car Wash

Marquis keeps talking. "My dad is thinking about opening a real car wash on Court Street around the corner from our house. He thinks our success on Saturdays shows we need a car wash around here. Jackson is going to work for him."

"Really?" I say as I put on an old T-shirt handed down from Jackson. "Well, Key, I hate to talk about my brother. I mean Jackson works hard and all, but your dad needs to keep him away from the money. He spends more than he has."

"What? How can he spend more than he has?" Marquis asks.

"By bouncing checks," I say as I shake my head.

"Okay, Jazz. My mom writes checks to pay bills. I never saw one bounce. They're made of paper."

"I know…because your mom only writes checks for less than or equal to the amount of money in her checking account at the bank. Jackson writes checks to people for *more* than he has in the bank. The bank sends the checks right back unpaid. That's why they call it a bounced check. Get it? Bounce back!"

"Got it. Jackson's got no money in the bank! So are they going to put him in jail?" Marquis asks. He seems fixated on jail. He's obviously been watching too much TV or hanging out with the wrong crowd. But maybe he's got a point. Bouncing checks may be considered stealing.

I look out the window again. "I don't know. But I know at least they'll charge him fees, close his checking account and make him pay for all the checks he wrote." I hear my mom calling me and Marquis to start washing cars. I quickly put on some old sneakers and say, "My granddad always said some people know how to make money, but don't know how to keep it." We crack up as we run outside.

CHAPTER 12

MY GRANDDAD'S PLAN

A few days later, me and Marquis wait for our ride home after football practice. It's great seeing my teammates before school starts in two weeks. But practice is brutal. The football field is about ten blocks from our house. We could walk, but we're too tired.

Marquis puts his helmet and pads on the ground. "Man, I'm too tired to meet Miss Benjamin now."

I put my helmet and pads down too. "Miss who?"

"Miss Benjamin, our banker." Marquis says. I forgot her name. How did Marquis know it? He sits on a rock next to my helmet. His dirty cleats dig into the ground to stop him from falling over.

"What do you mean our banker?"

"I didn't tell you?" Marquis looks up at me. "I opened a GAP account."

"A what? Are you speaking in code?"

"No...a GAP account: a Granddad Allowance Plan account. Get it? G for *Granddad*, A for *Allowance* and P for *Plan*. G-A-P. GAP. I made up that name. You see, I told my mom what your granddad said about getting an allowance the same as your age and saving it all. I told her that you got bank from that simple plan. She liked the idea. So now I get ten dollars a week. I'll be getting eleven dollars next week when I turn eleven. You remember next week is my birthday, right?"

I sit on the rock next to him. "Wow, Key. You're taking my granddad's advice? So you opened a youth savings account to put your allowance in, just like me?"

"Yep...and I told Miss Benjamin to name it the GAP account, after your granddad. She loved the idea. She and my mom set it up. So my allowance is taken from my mom's account and put directly into my savings account every week. Miss Benjamin calls it direct deposit. My mom likes it because she said she won't miss the money if it's taken out automatically. And it's less than her cell phone bill. So now the bank has ten GAP customers, including me and you! Miss Benjamin says some kids only get one dollar a week and some get more. But we all got bank, just like you. I'll have five thousand dollars saved by the time I'm eighteen years old."

Wow. I give Marquis a fist bump, then ask, "So why are you meeting *our* banker?" I like the way Marquis gets to know people. He can talk to anybody and makes friends so easily.

"I told Coach Wilson I would ask Miss Benjamin to sponsor our team by giving us a donation. The Tigers got Harold & Bell's restaurant to sponsor them. The Wildcats got Nubian Notions and they bought them new uniforms. Maybe the bank will sponsor us. Our uniforms are really tired. Do you want to come?" Marquis waves to his dad, gets up and grabs his stuff.

"Sure." I say as I grab my pad and helmet and follow him.

"Great! While we're there you can take some money out of your bank account for my birthday present. Remember...my birthday?"

I laugh. "Key, you know when my granddad said "save all of your allowance" he meant save it all. Maybe I can buy you a candy bar." I laugh again. Marquis turns around and tries to tackle me.

CHAPTER 13

MY SISTER

By the time I get home, I'm exhausted. I change out of my football practice uniform into some shorts and make my way into the living room. Jasmine is sitting on the sofa with her computer and watching TV at the same time. I look out the window at Wingate and think about going to find some friends. But it's too late. So I lie on the rug to watch TV, hoping Jasmine is watching BET. An ad comes on about the low, low prices at BJ Games Video Store.

I ask Jasmine, "Why don't we have a BJ Games around here? It seems like none of the stores on TV are in our neighborhood."

"I know," Jasmine says as she looks up at the TV. "I took the bus over to Gina's yesterday and she can walk to BJ Games from her house. You would love it in the north end. I wish Granddad had bought a house there instead of this one."

"Yeah...all we have on the south side are fast food restaurants and check cashing stores. I have to walk twenty blocks just to get

to the bank. Did you know that check cashing stores charge more than banks?"

Jasmine doesn't answer. So I keep talking. "We went to see Miss Benjamin at the bank to get her to sponsor the Raiders. I asked her why the bank is so far away but three check cashers are right up the street. She said that check cashers open stores here to rip us off. They charge high fees and get people to take out payday loans."

I Got Bank!

I sit up and look at Jasmine. "Do you know what a payday loan is?"

Jasmine stares at the TV and twists her braids like she doesn't know the answer. I lie back down, look at the ceiling and keep talking. "Miss Benjamin said a payday loan is when a check casher will lend you one hundred dollars on Monday and you have to pay back one hundred-ten dollars on Friday when you get paid. Well, one hundred-ten dollars doesn't seem like a lot, but the interest rate ends up being like nine hundred percent because they only gave you the money for four days! I only get paid three percent on my bank account. I think Mom only pays ten percent on her car loan. Nine hundred percent is a crazy high interest rate. I asked Miss Benjamin if check cashers are such a rip off, why does anybody use them. She said people don't know they're being ripped off and check cashers are close by. Can you believe that? Close by! Come on people...get in shape...walk twenty blocks to the bank...and get a calculator!"

Right then Jasmine bursts out crying. I jump up and look around thinking maybe I missed something. "What happen? Why are you crying?"

Jasmine runs into the kitchen. I dive back down on the floor thinking maybe something came through the window. I start crawling toward the kitchen when Jasmine walks back in with a paper towel, wiping her face and says, "I didn't know check cashers charge so much interest or that I'd had to pay back so much money."

I look at Jasmine. I'm shocked. "Jasmine, you got a payday loan? You don't even have a job?" I slowly get up off the floor.

"I couldn't wait for the one hundred-fifty dollars from working at the car wash to pay for my concert tickets," she says as she waves the damp paper towel in the air. "The concert would've been sold out. So I got a loan from up the street at Quick Check Cashers."

I'm still shocked. I stand over her and my hands just start waving in the air, while I say, "Jasmine, you're only fifteen. You don't have a job. How did you get a payday loan?"

"They call it an allowance loan," she says as she buries her face into the towel. "But they didn't tell me that I would be paying them back for the rest of my life!"

CHAPTER 14

MAKING MONEY

The following week of practice wears me and Marquis out. There are drills, drills and more drills. We lay on the grass using our helmets as pillows, waiting for our ride home. Most of our teammates are waiting too. Our coach catches all the parents when they drive up to remind them about the weigh-in next week.

"So Jazz, my dad is really excited about starting a car wash. He found a place on Court Street," Marquis says as he adjusts his helmet behind his head.

"Great! Does he know how a car wash makes money?" I ask.

Marquis laughs. "Yeah...washing cars!"

"No, Key, I don't mean what happens at a car wash, I mean how it makes money." Marquis looks at me like he's confused.

I sit up. "You see, my granddad and I would play this game called how in the world does this place make money? Anytime we walked into a business, we would ask ourselves, 'How in the world does this place make money?' It was fun. And it taught me a lot."

I GOT BANK!

"Yeah, like what?" Marquis asks.

"Well." I say and lie back down. "The first thing it taught me is to *always* ask the question."

"Okay Jazz." Marquis sits up. "How does McDonald's make money? Selling hamburgers, right?"

I laugh. "Not really. McDonalds makes money from selling food, but it makes more money selling drinks!" I say. Marquis looks like he's shocked. I continue. "Yeah…a soda only costs about five cents, and they sell it for over one dollar. While a hamburger might cost one dollar and they sell it for ninety-nine cents. Also, McDonalds gets money for food and drinks, but they have to pay for the people who work there, the food, the buildings and TV ads. If they don't keep their cost down, they won't make any money. That's why they hire kids for low pay and train them to always ask, 'Do you want a drink with your order?' Or they get them to order those meals that come with a drink."

"Wow Jazz!" Marquis says and sits on his knees. "Okay, what about a bank? How does a bank make money? From our savings account?"

Funny he would ask this question. I had just asked Miss Benjamin the other day. "No. A savings account costs them money because they pay us interest. I think you get an interest rate of one percent on your GAP account. Right?" Marquis nods. "Okay, so the bank takes money into savings accounts, then lends the money to people to buy homes, cars and other things. Like my mom pays an interest rate of ten percent on her car loan. So the bank gets paid ten percent on my mom's loan but only pays you one percent on your savings account. So ten percent minus one percent—they get the nine percent difference plus they charge for stuff. They call it fees. Then they pay for the people, buildings and other stuff. The difference between what comes in and what goes out is how they make money. It's called profit."

"Wow, Jazz! I got it. So let me think. A car wash gets paid money for washing cars, but it has to pay for the people, the building, the water and soap. So it has to keep those costs down to make money." Marquis jumps to his feet and looks at me. "So that's why your mom only paid us ten dollars to wash all those cars every Saturday. That's how she was making money! Hmmm…I better talk to my dad, because there's no way I'm washing any more cars!"

CHAPTER 15

IT'S A CRIME

It took me a few days to get over seeing Jasmine crying about the check casher. Now I know I have to find the key to get my family to the other side—where there is money, success and happiness like I see on TV. So I walk twenty blocks to meet my banker, Miss Benjamin. While I sit in one of the chairs waiting for her, I look around the bank. I see that a bank branch is like an office. It has people working at desks like Miss Benjamin and it has a place to sit and wait. I check out the people standing behind the bullet-proof glass. They don't look as mean as they did the first time I came here. Now I know that the glass is to prevent bank robberies. I think about Marquis, who knows everybody here by name. I also see I'm the only kid in the bank.

"Hi Jazz," Miss Benjamin says. "How can I help you today?"

I look up to see Miss Benjamin standing over me. Now that

she's not sitting at her desk, I can see that she's very tall. She's wearing a blue suit, looking like a banker. I stand up and follow her to her desk.

"I'm not sure if you can help me this time," I say.

"Well, let me try."

I sit down and say, "Okay. My sister Jasmine, who is only fifteen, took out a one- hundred-fifty dollar payday loan to go to a concert."

"That can't be," Miss Benjamin says as she raises her eyebrows. "You have to be eighteen or older to get a loan. Did your mother sign for the loan?"

"No. They call it an allowance loan and she has to give them her entire allowance for one year to pay back the loan. I told her she should've just saved her money or not gone to the concert. But now she has to pay Quick Check Cashers fifteen dollars a week for one year which adds up to seven hundred-eighty dollars for a one hundred-fifty loan. That seems like too much money. I think they're ripping her off!"

"Wait. Wait Jazz. You're talking too fast. Are you sure your sister has a payday...no... an allowance loan from Quick Check Cashers?" Miss Benjamin asks as she leans over and looks at me very seriously.

"Yes."

"Well. It's a crime to lend money to kids," she says. "If you think a check cashing store or bank did something wrong you should report them to the police, the state banking office and the FDIC."

"The who? Do you mean the FBI?" I think Miss Benjamin is confused.

"No. I mean the Federal Deposit Insurance Corporation or FDIC for short. They make sure banks follow banking rules and make sure people don't lose money in their bank account. The FDIC protects your deposit. The state banking office watches over check cashing stores to make sure they follow the rules. And the police make sure everyone follows the law. It's wrong to give a loan to anyone under eighteen. And yes, it's wrong to pay back seven-hundred-eighty dollars for a one hundred-fifty dollar one-year loan."

"Okay...so can my sister send Quick Check Cashers to jail?" I ask. I'm starting to think about jail all the time like Marquis.

I Got Bank!

"Well, she can at least have them stop giving loans to kids," Miss Benjamin says back.

"Okay," I say. "So she should call the police, the state banking office and the FDIC." Miss Benjamin nods. I stand up to leave, but then stop. "One more thing..." I say to Miss Benjamin as I look around the bank. "Where are the kids?"

"Excuse me?" Miss Benjamin asks as though she didn't hear the question.

"I've been in this bank branch many times and I'm always the only kid here. If kids can't go to check cashers and they're not in a bank, where are they?" I ask as I raise my hands up in the air.

Miss Benjamin frowns. "I agree Jazz. We need more kids to have bank accounts. Maybe I can come to your school to talk to your class about banking. Can you ask your teacher?"

"Sure. My teacher would like that," I say as I leave.

CHAPTER 16
LITTLE RED CORVETTE

"Hey losers," Jackson says to me and Marquis as he sits down with us at the kitchen table. As usual, my older brother is dressed in the latest clothes and looks like he just came from a video shoot. "Do you want to see my new ride?" He puts a magazine on the table. I look at Marquis. Marquis looks at the magazine.

"That's my car, a deluxe convertible with a V8 engine and a smooth ride. See those rims?" Jackson points to a red car with tan leather seats and chrome rims. The ad says, 'For the one who has it all.'

"Jazz, did Marquis tell you that I'm opening a car wash with his dad?" He looks at me, then at Marquis. "Soon I'm going to have so much money that I'll be able to buy everything! I might even buy you two some video games, if you're lucky. But first, I'm buying this new car!"

I Got Bank!

Marquis takes the magazine and shows it to Jazz. "Man! This car is sweet!"

I look at the ad. Even though I love the car, something doesn't smell right. For some reason, I don't believe Jackson has found the key to money, success and happiness. "Jackson," I call out. "This ad says for the one who has it all. That's not you."

Jackson laughs. "Yeah, well it will be me when I buy this car." His cell phone rings. He jumps up while he answers it, grabs the magazine and leaves the room.

I watch Jackson leave, then say to Marquis, "My granddad always said that if you see somebody with a fancy new car, but no house, they got no money in the bank." I put my head down on the table. "Dang, that's turning out to be my brother."

CHAPTER 17

GRANDMA'S HANDS

A few weeks later, on a cold fall afternoon, me, Marquis and our teammates are on a bus headed home from our second football game of the season. We won by two touchdowns! Marquis kicked a field goal, which Coach Wilson said is a big deal for an eleven-year-old. Marquis is very excited. Everybody is tired. The game was played out in the burbs, a long way from our neighborhood. On the bus ride home, I like looking out of the window into people's houses. There are so many nice homes. I'm asking myself how they all seem to have found the key and I can't find it.

"I can't wait to tell my dad about the game," Marquis leans forward and says to me. I'm sitting in the seat in front of him. "Too bad he had to work today."

As the bus waits at a stop sign, I see a family sitting at the table eating dinner. They look so comfortable—like on TV. The bus takes off and I catch the end of Marquis' comment. "He'll catch the next game." I say. "Maybe next time you'll kick two field goals!" I smile as I look back at him. "What's going on with the car wash, anyway?"

I Got Bank!

"Well, my dad found a place on Court Street that has low rent. He also found workers. He put an ad in the paper looking for people who want to work part time because they cost less. All these grandmothers applied for the jobs. So I told him to name the place Grandma's Hand Car Wash. That way people will know that their car is in good hands and he can charge twenty dollars for a wash."

"Wow! He should make a lot of money," I say. But I saw Marquis staring out the window like he was far, far away.

"Yeah, but Great National Bank wouldn't give him the loan he needs to get started." Marquis says. "They said that most new businesses fail because they don't make enough money. They also said since he has never owned a car wash and doesn't have experience running a car wash, they couldn't lend him the money. So I think the car wash is dead." He frowns. I turn back around and look out the window. I notice the houses have changed to mostly apartment buildings. I can tell we're getting close to home.

I turn back around again and ask Marquis, "Don't your mom and dad own your house?" Marquis looks at me and nods his head. "Well they can use your house as collateral."

"Collateral?" Marquis asks. "What's that again?"

"Collateral is something of value like a house that can be used to repay a loan. If you take out a loan with collateral and you don't pay the loan back, the bank can take the collateral and sell it to get their money back. So, they're more willing to give you a loan if you have collateral. With your house, maybe Miss Benjamin will give your dad a loan to start the car wash."

"Yeah...great idea. I'll tell my dad," Marquis says then pauses. "He can tell my mom. I'm not sure she'll like her house being collateral. I think the name Grandma's Hand Car Wash is going to change to Mama Said This Better Work Out Car Wash." We crack up.

42

CHAPTER 18

WHO TEACHES KIDS?

Jazz Ellington
September 30

Granddad, I wish you were here. You were right that if I want to be successful I got to have bank. I mean, everyday it seems like something comes up that has to do with money. We need new football uniforms. Key's dad needs money to start their new car wash. Jasmine needs money to pay back her allowance loan. Mom always needs money...and Jackson wants things that cost money he doesn't even have. Every time, I keep asking "Got Bank?" "Got Bank?" And the answer is no! I'm so glad that I get an allowance the same as my age...and save it all...so I got bank...over two thousand dollars! But I don't understand if money is so important, why nobody but you...and Miss Benjamin...teaches kids. And how can money be the key to success and happiness—like on TV—if nobody I know has money? Makes no sense. Anyway, I used the money I got from the car wash last summer and went with Key to BJ Games. The store is huge with tons of video games and really low prices and there were only two other kids in the store. So I asked myself, how in the world does BJ Games make money? Their costs seem too high. And guess what? On the news tonight it said that BJ Games is going out of business. I was right on the money!

PART 3

WINTER BLUES WITH
OTHER PEOPLE'S MONEY

CHAPTER 19

ALL MONEY IS NOT GOOD

I lean my head against the cold bus window and think TGIF. Thank God Its Friday, and school is over for the week. We only have two weekends free before basketball season starts. I'm going to play video games or be on the computer nonstop all weekend long, or at least until my mom puts an end to it. The bus is freezing. Even the bus driver is blowing into his hands at every stop to stay warm.

"Jazz, come to Scrub-Away with me tomorrow to count cars," Marquis says.

"Key, are you crazy? It's freezing out." I look at my best friend. "Why are you counting cars at Scrub-Away anyway?"

"Man...it's my mom. She has us counting cars at different car washes all over town to see how much money they make. Once my dad told her that the bank would only give him a loan to open a car wash if he agreed to use our house as collateral, she went nuts. First, she asked us if we knew that using our house as collateral means if we don't pay back the loan, the bank will sell our house to get their money back. I said...yeah, I know what collateral means."

I Got Bank!

Marquis looks at me like, of course he knows. "I told her that a bank is more willing to give you a loan if you have collateral—something of value like a house or a car. And you know what she said?"

"No...what?" I ask while I smile at him.

"She said that just because they'll *give* you a loan doesn't mean you should *take* it. Can you believe that? I mean...hello. Why wouldn't you take the money?"

I start to laugh until I see his frustration. "Well your mom probably doesn't want to end up like Jasmine. I mean she took out a one hundred-fifty pay day loan from Quick Check Cashers and she has to pay them back seven hundred-eighty dollars!"

"Jazz, what are you talking about? How can your sister take out a pay day loan? Isn't she fifteen? Does she even have a job? And why does she have to pay back so much money? Sounds like a rip off."

"Yeah...they call it an allowance loan. It's a long story. We're going to report Quick Check Cashers to the police. But my point is... well...my granddad always said "*All* money is not good money." Your mom is right to make sure you know what you're getting into before you take out a loan. Maybe she's not sure it's a good idea to use your house as collateral to start a new car wash."

"Yeah...it's clear she's not sure. We've been counting cars for the past three weeks. She and my dad have been sitting in front of the computer adding up the car counts and going over the budget. And they've been arguing a lot. With everybody! They say they're negotiating, but it sounds like arguing to me. They seem so excited and the car wash is *all* they talk about. It's really weird."

The bus gets to our stop. Marquis gets up and follows me. "So... this is my last day of counting cars. If you come, it'll go faster and we can go to BJ Games when we're done. They're having a going-out-of-business sale."

I hear BJ Games and remember I still have money from my birthday. Finally Marquis says something that makes some sense. "Cool...I'll go."

CHAPTER 20

RECYCLING

On Monday, I walk in my class and see this tall woman in a gray suit talking to my teacher. It's Miss Benjamin, my banker. I totally forgot she was coming to my class. I take my seat quickly.

"Hi Jazz," she says, way too loudly. "I was just talking to Mrs. Farrar about you." I see my entire class look at me. Definitely not cool. Why did I think it was a good idea to invite her to class?

"Okay everyone, take your seat. We have a visitor today," Mrs. Farrar says. I sit way down in my seat hoping Visiting Day will be over soon.

"Hi everyone, my name is Miss Benjamin and I'm a banker. Does anyone know what a banker is?" A few kids raise their hands. She looks at me like she expects me to answer. I don't even think about raising my hand. She points to Noah who is sitting by the window.

"Somebody who works at a bank," he says and laughs. The class laughs with him. Miss Benjamin smiles and points to Tisha sitting in the front row.

I Got Bank!

"Someone who cashes checks and gives people money," Tisha says.

"Yes, when people take money from their bank account, it's called a withdrawal. A banker *does* do withdrawals and cash checks. But I'm wondering if anyone knows what a banker *is*. Does anyone know what a banker *is*?" More hands go up. A lot of kids in my class would love to beat Tisha. She's always right. Miss Benjamin points to Ramon in the back.

"You count money at a bank...like Great National Bank. And you help people save."

"Yes. When people put money into their bank account it's called a deposit. A banker *does* take in deposits to help people save money. However, a banker *is* a recycler. Does anyone know what recycle means?" She looks at all the raised hands then points to Hasan in the back.

"Yeah, recycle means taking stuff like cans and bringing them to the store so you get money back and they can use the cans again."

"That's right. When you recycle, you use something over again, right?" Everybody nods. "So a banker is someone who takes in money from people in our community who want to save. Then the banker uses that money. As a minority bank, Community Unity Bank recycles that money back into our community by giving people loans to buy houses and to grow businesses. So a banker is a recycler, except we recycle money instead of cans. Now...why do we need a recycler? Why should we recycle?" She points to Nyla in the front.

"Because we don't want to waste things that we can use again and it's good to recycle."

"That's right...we don't want to throw *everything* away because some things we can use again. We don't want too much waste. So... if everyone threw *all* the cans away or spent *all* their money, would that be a good thing?" Everybody said no. "That's right. We need to save some things to take care of our community."

"So, how many of you get an allowance?" About half the class raises their hands. "Okay. How many of you get birthday money, soda money, money for doing chores, lunch money or any money at

I Got Bank!

all?" All thirty kids raise their hands high. "Great! Now...how many of you have a savings account?" All hands come down, except for three kids including me. "Hmm? So what's happening with *all* your money? Why aren't you recycling?" Everybody laughs and so does Miss Benjamin.

Visiting Day continues and Miss Benjamin is great. She talks about her first savings account. She wanted to spend *all* her money on new clothes, but her dad told her she needed to give some money to church and save some money so that one day she could buy something really big. She talks about when her daughter, Serena, was born. Miss Benjamin spent too much money and messed up her credit cards. She had to move back in with her parents and come up with a budget. It took her years to fix her credit and then become a banker. She says that even when things were really tough, she never lost faith. Then she talks about when she got back on her feet and bought her house... how she and her daughter ran from room to room screaming "This is ours, all ours!" And she talks about how saving money can make you happy and spending *more* money than you have can make you sad. Then she gives everybody I Got Bank! stickers.

The kids love her. I'm glad she came.

CHAPTER 21

I'M NOT A ROOMMATE

"Hey Jazz," Jackson says as he comes in the kitchen and looks around. "Is Mom home?"

I look at my big brother and notice his new sneakers. "No, she went with Jasmine to some meeting."

"Good. I'm expecting a call from a car dealer. I told him I live with some roommates. So, if you answer the phone, tell him you're my roommate."

"What?" I jump up from the table. "Are you crazy? I'm not going to lie. I probably don't even sound like somebody's roommate."

"Yeah...you're right. Okay, just say you're my roommate's little brother." He must have picked up my annoyance. "Look Jazz. I'm trying to get a loan to buy a new car. You know the red convertible that I showed you and Marquis in the magazine. The car is really hard to find and this dealer has one. He knows I'm still in school, but he also knows I'll be opening a new car wash with Marquis' dad soon. He just wants to confirm my place of residence—where I live. Then he can come get the car if I don't pay back my loan. But that's not going to happen. So...maybe...just don't answer the phone."

"Jackson, can't you get in trouble for lying to people? And did Key's mom agree to the loan for the car wash?"

"What? I don't know a thing about a loan. But I do know the car wash will be open soon, I'll have my new car and you'll have the coolest brother in town." The phone rings. "Jackson Ellington here, how can I help you? Oh...hi Mister Green." He walks into the living room with the phone. I'm so annoyed; I go to my room and slam my door.

CHAPTER 22

OTHER PEOPLE'S MONEY

Jazz Ellington
December 15

Granddad...I wish you were here. I've been thinking about you a lot lately. Remember when you told me, "If you're not willing to spend your money on what you want, it's not worth wanting." Well, at the time I had no idea what you were talking about. And remember when I asked you to buy me that new Sky Ranger and you told me that you would pay half, if I paid half? Well, I said no because I thought you were just being stingy. Now I know that what you were trying to say is that it's easy to want something if you're using other people's money. Jackson is trying to get other people's money to buy a new car that he doesn't even need. I mean he never even leaves the neighborhood. And he doesn't even have a job yet! He thinks he's going to open a car wash, but Key's mom isn't sure she wants to open the car wash because if it doesn't work, they could lose their house. So I'm thinking about telling Mom that Jackson is a fake, buying a new car with no money in the bank. But I don't want to be a snitch. Maybe I'll just have to deal with Jackson myself.

By the way, you were right. I really didn't want that Sky Ranger.

CHAPTER 23

THE PO PO!

The door slams and Marquis comes running in the house yelling, "Jazz...Jasmine. Come quick." I run from the kitchen and Jasmine runs from her room.

"What's up?" I ask as I see Marquis peering out the front window.

"You're not going to believe it. The cops are taking over Quick Check Cashers. I mean they're all over the place," Marquis yells as he runs back out the door. Me and Jasmine grab our coats and run after him.

Two blocks away, we see a crowd standing in front of Quick Check Cashers and flashing blue lights bouncing off the windows. There are so many people I can't see what's going on. We try to make our way to the front of the crowd.

I get to the front first. A policeman stands right in front of me so I can't see much. All I see is a lot of police inside of Quick Check Cashers. Two carry boxes out and place them in a van. Another seems to be guarding the van.

THE PO PO!

It takes Marquis a long time to get to the front because he stops to talk to everybody he knows. TMT! When he finally gets to the front, he says hey to somebody named Derek, standing next to me, checking out the scene too. "Hey, Marquis. Man, it sure seems like a lot of cops for a robbery," Derek says. "I mean...I haven't seen this many cops in our neighborhood since that cop got shot two years ago."

An older man standing close by says, "They weren't robbed. They're terrorists. Taking drug money and sending it overseas. I heard it on the news. The owner was arrested downtown and the police are here taking evidence. Boy, I hope they processed my telephone bill I paid this morning before the police showed up." I then hear Marquis asking him a bunch of questions. I just watch the whole scene.

Then Jasmine finally joins us. Now she starts talking. Says she went with Mom to the police station to file a police report about her loan from Quick Check Cashers. She learned that lending money to somebody under eighteen is against the law. Says she never saw Mom so angry. The policewoman was angry too. She thought Mom and the policewoman were going to leave the station, go to Quick Check Cashers and give somebody the beat down. Because they filed the report, she didn't have to make any more loan payments. But she didn't want anybody at Quick Check Cashers to go to jail. She feels awful. So Jasmine thinks she's the reason why the police are here.

"I promise I will never take out another loan for as long as I live," she says over and over. I think she's praying. I can't decide if I should tell her they may be money laundering or supporting terrorists. Or maybe they were robbed. I'm not sure which, but I know the police aren't here because of her one-hundred-fifty dollar loan. For some reason, I don't think she wants to hear that.

By the time the three of us go home the police are gone and Quick Check Cashers is closed. Marquis tries to tell me about the drug money going overseas and the owner who might be a terrorist. Jasmine says she just wants to go to bed.

CHAPTER 24

WARRIORS

After my basketball game, I watch the high school kids play. I can already tell who is going to get a basketball scholarship and even who might go pro. They have something special. It could be height. Or size. Or strength and quick moves. But they also stand out from the other kids because they have more courage... they play harder and smarter when they are in a tough game or when their team is losing. My granddad always called them "warriors." He told me to be really good at something, you have to be a warrior. You have to be tough when you're down.

Thinking about my granddad reminds me of Mister David. It was cool meeting somebody who knew my granddad, back in the day. I met him last night at Marquis' house. Mrs. Hill, Marquis' mom, invited me to join their Kitchen Cabinet meeting. That's their

dinner on Friday nights to talk about starting their new car wash. I found out they've been meeting since last summer: Mister and Mrs. Hill, Mr. David and another man and woman.

Mr. David looks strange. He's a small older man with all these grooves in his face that make him look ancient. And he has very large hands. But more than his looks, he tells great stories. He says that back in the day, Granddad was the best chef in town...how people would cry tears of joy when they ate his food. He learned to cook when he was in the army in Europe. Mr. David says that every fancy restaurant up and down the coast wanted to hire Granddad, but he was very choosey about where he worked. And he believed in supporting Black businesses. So he worked at Mahogany Cafe and Grill. Said Granddad was a class act.

Mrs. Hill says that Mr. David is a famous auto mechanic, fixing a lot of luxury cars. She says his customers have been coming to his shop from miles away for over forty years. He says it's because he treats automobiles with the respect they deserve. He calls the automobile the most important invention of the twentieth century. When Mister David talks, I feel like my granddad is in the room. He has the same way of making everybody in the room better. Marquis wanted to leave the table to go play video games, but I just wanted to stay and listen. Marquis is lucky to have this experience every Friday night.

At the end of the night, Mr. Hill invites me to come back any-time...and maybe I can convince Jackson to come too. He says although Jackson will have a job at the car wash, maybe he can learn more about the business if he comes to their meetings. He has been inviting Jackson since last summer and is about to give up on him coming. I promise to try talking him into coming. Something tells me he's not going to listen.

CHAPTER 25

OPENING DAY

"Come on Jazz," Jasmine yells. "You're taking too long." She waits by the door for me to find my coat. .

After many months of research and discussion and Mister and Mrs. Hill taking out a loan, it's finally opening day for Grandma's Hand Car Wash! The Kitchen Cabinet decided January would be a great time to open because bad weather makes cars dirty. Jackson and Marquis, along with Mister and Mrs. Hill and all the grand-mothers on the car wash team are already there. Jasmine wakes me up at six o'clock to tell me she wants to leave at seven. I'm sur-prised she's so excited. The car wash doesn't open until eight.

By the time we get close to the car wash at seven-fifteen, I can't believe my eyes. There are cars lined up around the block waiting to be washed. "Looks like the whole deacon board and the choir are in line. I see Reverend Haywood too!" Jasmine says.

"You know all these people?" I ask. I only recognize Reverend Haywood.

I Got Bank!

"Sure...dummy!" Jasmine says. "I think Mister and Mrs. Hill went to every church in town telling them how they want to hire from our community and build a business the community can be proud of. They also went to all the mechanics in town to let them know their customers would be in good hands. I think they talked to everybody who'd listen. You can see where Marquis gets it from. That's one talking family!"

When we reach the car wash, I see my brother checking all the equipment and making sure everybody is ready. "Hey Jazz and Jasmine," he says. "Glad you came early. We may need your help. Can you believe this line? We're going to open early so that people don't have to wait. Everybody ready?" he yells to his team of workers.

"Yeah," everybody yells back. And Grandma's Hand Car Wash opens!

CHAPTER 26

WHO'S GOT BANK?

A few weeks later, I see Marquis at the bus stop and can tell he's still tired from our weekend of basketball. We lost our last game of the tournament. I was tired and bummed out too until I listened to the radio while I was eating breakfast.

"Hey Key," I say. "I heard Grandma's Hand Car Wash on KJLH this morning. They said after three weeks in business, you have more customers than Scrub-Away, which has been in business for over twenty-five years!"

"Yeah, but it's a lot of work. My dad says he's working harder than when he worked for somebody else. I mean...Jackson gets to go home when we close at night. My dad is up late finding ways to make the next day better. My mom is up late finding ways to pay back the loan quicker. I can't even play on the computer any more because they hog it all night. And my mom is still working at the hospital part time. They're both working around the clock."

"Well, at least the car wash is making enough money to pay back the loan," I say. We both laugh. "I'm amazed that Jackson can

sleep at night. He never has enough money to make his car loan payments. My mom says he needs a budget. I think they may repo his car."

"Repo? What's repo?" Marquis asks me.

"Repossess. The bank or car lender will come in the middle of the night and take the car back if Jackson doesn't make his loan payments. The car is the lender's collateral, so they'll take back the car and sell it to get their money back if Jackson doesn't pay them."

"Wow! That sounds like my mom. She's always worried that things won't work out and we won't be able to pay back the mortgage loan they took out to open the car wash. I guess she doesn't want the bank to repo our house!"

"Yeah...but Key...they can't repo your house. I mean they can't come in the middle of the night and take your house away. But they can foreclose, which means throw you out and sell your house to somebody else to get their money back. Good thing the car wash is working. But Jackson may be facing the repo man."

"Wow," Marquis says. "It's such a sweet ride. My dad tells him to park it in front of the car wash to attract new customers."

As we get on the bus, Kenny calls us to the back and says, "Jazz…I like your brother's new car. You think he'll take me for a ride?"

I whisper to Marquis "If he doesn't face the repo man first." We both crack up. Kenny frowns at us like we're laughing at him.

He yells, "What are you laughing at Marquis? Jackson gave everybody in your family a job. I'm just looking for a ride."

"What?" I say. Kenny's words seem so jumbled I can't understand what he's saying.

Kenny keeps talking as though he's talking to everybody on the bus. "Jackson is going to open car washes all over town and one day I'm going to work for him. Marquis, you just better hope Jackson doesn't fire your momma." At that point, Marquis lunges at Kenny, ready to fight. Nobody talks about his mom.

I have to hold him back and I say "Hold up, Key. He's clearly an idiot." Marquis looks at me and backs off.

We go to the front of the bus and sit down, then crack up laughing. I say, "Can you believe he thinks because Jackson has a new ride he *owns* the car wash. He doesn't even own the *car*! It's just like my granddad said, "You can't always tell who's 'got bank' by how they look."

Marquis laughs and says, "Yeah. And he's counting on *Jackson* for a job? And I was going to risk getting suspended for *him*? Man, I need to keep my cool and he needs to get a savings plan."

"For real!" I respond and give Marquis a fist bump.

PART 4
GIVING INTO SPRING

Chapter 27

Gospel Rap

When I walk up to my front door, I can tell Jasmine is home early from school. Weird music is blasting from the living room and I can hear her friends laughing and somebody talking on the computer. I try to duck from the living room into the kitchen to avoid the scene, but the kitchen door is blocked. I'm trapped.

"Hi Jazz," they all say together like a choir. I have no choice but to face them.

"Hi," I say as I look around the room and try to figure out the music blasting. I always wonder why Jasmine likes such weird music. She likes rap and hip hop, but she also likes jazz, rock and gospel music. The music blasting sounds like gospel, but with a rapper! Her friends are also weird. There are big ones and little ones, black ones and white ones. The only thing they seem to have in common is their age—about sixteen years old like Jasmine. I recognize Gina and Chelsea, but the others are just a blur. And books are everywhere...boxes and boxes of books. I need to escape. "Jasmine, I'm

I GOT BANK!

going over to Key's house. Mom already knows. I'll be home around eight." I step over boxes through the living room to my room.

I hear Jasmine explaining me to her friends, like she always does. "His best friend's family owns Grandma's Hand Car Wash. Every Friday night they have a Kitchen Cabinet meeting to talk about ways to make it better. It seems to be going great to me. I don't know why they keep meeting."

I tune out the rest. I close my door, throw down my back pack and fall on my bed. Glad my mom finally removed the top bunk. After a few minutes, I change my sweatshirt. Then I hear a knock on my door.

"Jazz, before you go, we need your advice," Jasmine says through the door. I'm thinking...what now? I crack open the door and Jasmine says, "It'll only take a few minutes. We're trying to decide how to display the books and we'd like your advice on the best books for kids your age." When people say things I don't expect, the words sound jumbled. Sort of like Kenny the other day. I must have looked confused, so Jasmine says, "Just come look." She turns around and walks toward the kitchen. I follow her without knowing why.

Nothing she said could have prepared me for what I see when I walk in the kitchen. Piled on top of every flat surface—from the table, to the counters, to the chair seats...to even the refrigerator— are tons and tons of books. I could feel my eyes get big, like I'm having an out of body experience. I look on the floor and there are books there too! Some of the girls from the living room are now standing in the kitchen doorway and they're all looking at me.

I try to speak calmly, even though my mind is racing. "Where did all these books come from?" I look at my sister.

"They were donated. People gave them to us for free," she says.

"Somebody *gave* you all these books? For free? Why? Are you having a book sale?" Finally, I got it. Just like in school, they're having a book sale!

"No. We're going to give them away," one of the weird girls says. I squint, trying to figure out which weird girl spoke.

"To who...why?" I ask. I look more closely and see many books I've read or want to read. I see Sky Ranger comic books that were my favorite when I was younger. My granddad used to read them to me. I see *The Boondocks* comic books—my granddad's favorite. I see all kinds of book series. I also see some "girly" books that I always hated. I try to add up the cost of all the books and the numbers get too big for me to add up in my head. I try to imagine what's going to happen to all these books. Another weird girl speaks.

"We're giving them away for free at the fair in a few weeks. Haven't you heard of the Yancey Book Fair?"

That was one weird comment too many. Now I know it's time for me to leave. "No and I have to go. Sorry, I can't help you." And I back out of the kitchen, jump over boxes of books in the living room and run out the door for Marquis' house.

CHAPTER 28

COMPETITION

"What's up, Jazz," Mr. Hill says when I walk in and smell my favorite food, home-made macaroni and cheese. "Can you get Marquis out of his room? Let him know that dinner is ready." I run to the back of the house and find Marquis playing a video game.

"Hey Key, your dad said dinner is ready." Marquis doesn't look up. He has one more lap before the race ends. I watch as Marquis wins the race then pauses the game.

"What's up Money?" Marquis lightly punches me on the arm.

"Key, I'm so glad to be here. My house has been invaded by the weirdest girls I've ever seen. And they must have over one thousand books!"

"What? In your house? Must be something Jasmine is doing." We walk to the kitchen.

When we sit down to eat, we hear Mister David arguing loudly with Mrs. Hill. "Look Lena. Just because Scrub-Away is coming to our neighborhood, doesn't mean you should pack up and run away. When Auto-Mechanic came ten years ago, everyone told me that I was through…that my business was going to dry up. It didn't happen."

"I'm not saying run away," Mrs. Hill argues back as she places food on the table and motions to me and Marquis to get up and wash our hands. "But if they come, it's going to hurt our business. Some of our customers are going to leave us to save ten dollars a wash. It doesn't matter that Scrub-Away's automatic car washer doesn't clean as well as our hand washing. In our neighborhood, ten dollars is a lot of money."

Me and Marquis look at each other, shocked to hear Scrub-Away is coming. Grandma's Hand Car Wash has been open for four months now and business is booming. There have been many news stories about its success. All the news must have caught the attention of Scrub-Away, a company with many car washes around town. Customers drive through their building and machines automatically wash their cars. Now Scrub-Away is going to invade our neighborhood. We wash our hands quickly and sit down to hear more. Mrs. Hill sits down too and looks very concerned.

"Well, I think we should focus on solutions instead of the problem," says Mr. Hill as he takes a piece of chicken and hands the platter to Marquis. Everybody looks at him. "They can't compete with our service—the way Jackson personally greets customers when they drive up and the way he makes sure our employees care for their cars. Jazz, your brother is great with people," he says as he passes me the macaroni and cheese. I dig into the mac 'n cheese and think about how everybody at the car wash always gets excited when they see Jackson.

"So we just need to focus on our price," Mr. Hill continues. "And the way I see it, we have three choices. We can reduce our price from twenty dollars to ten dollars." I watch the table shake their head no. "We can try a frequent user program, like buy four washes and get one for free. That way, people can pay eighty dollars for five car washes or sixteen dollars a wash." The table seems to like that idea better, but we all wait to hear the third choice. "Or we can just call Scrub-Away, ask them to buy us out and hand them our keys and they can move into our location." We all look at Mr. Hill like he has lost his mind.

CHAPTER 29

HEAT OF THE NIGHT

A few nights later, I'm finding it hard to sleep again. Its springtime and I'm so excited that summer is coming that I can almost taste it. I lie in my bed and dream about all the things I'm going to do when I no longer have homework, tests and teachers. Last summer I played at the Boys & Girls Club all week and worked at the car wash on Saturdays. Glad my mom's car loan got paid off. This year Coach Wilson got me a scholarship to go with Marquis to sleep away camp for two weeks.

Marquis said we're going to be attacked by bears and other animals in our cabin at camp. I'm not afraid of a thing in the street... but a bear? As I doze off, I could almost hear the bear breathing and growling in the woods. His growl gets louder as he moves in closer. His huge size creates a dark cloud over the camp. I try to convince myself that it's just a bad dream, but I can feel the fear as everybody starts screaming and running around trying to get away from the bear. I think maybe it's not a dream. I push myself to get out of bed. I fall on the floor, hard. Dang! I get up and try to grab my sweat shirt, but the cabin is confusing. It's so familiar, but also feels strange. It's so dark. I raise my head and hear the bear growling and my mom screaming. My mom? The bear is attacking my mom? What's she doing at camp anyway?

I run through the cabin door to rescue her and see Jackson and Jasmine running around. Jackson? Jasmine?

"Jackson. How could you let this happen? Why didn't you tell me you couldn't pay your bills?" I hear Mom yelling, but it doesn't make any sense. It's that jumbled sound again.

"I can't believe they took my car! I can't believe they took my car! How can they just come take my car? This is messed up." I hear Jackson repeat over and over again. Finally I wake up. This is worse than a bad dream. This is real. They've repossessed Jackson's car. Came to our house—in the heat of the night—and took his car...no, not *his* car...took *their* car back because Jackson didn't make his car loan payments. It wasn't a bear. It was the repo man.

CHAPTER 30

I'M TOO POOR

Weeks later, me and Marquis are lying on the floor playing video games. It's a two-player racing game, but the split screen annoys us. We prefer to take turns. I watch Marquis guide his car around the track at fast speeds. Our coach says Marquis has great hand-to-eye coordination, which is why he is such a great athlete. During the spring, I rarely see him because he plays two sports— baseball and spring soccer. He came over today to show off his bank statement. After about a year, Marquis had saved over four hundred dollars and likes showing it off. His show-and-tell lasted one minute before we ran off to play video games.

"Hey Marquis," Jasmine says as she walks in my room without knocking.

"Hey Jasmine," Marquis looks at her and takes his eyes off the screen. His car crashes into a wall, flips over and explodes. "Ah, man," he complains and tosses the controller.

"Jasmine, can't you see we're busy," I yell at my sister.

"Okay, but this will only take a minute." Jasmine sits on top of my desk. "I'd like you two to give a one hundred dollar donation to the Yancey Book Fair. We give away new books to children in our community to encourage them to read. Many of them are reading below grade level and don't have any books in their homes. If you could see their joy when they receive a new book they can call their own, you'd know the gift is priceless. And if everyone, like you two, gives a little to the fair, we'll be able to make more kids happy. And we can encourage kids in our community to read more."

I look to see if my sister is reading a script. She sounds like a commercial...like she's practiced this speech over and over again.

I Got Bank!

I thought, where's the replay button? I stopped listening once she asked for one hundred dollars! Then I thought again. Where's the escape button?

"Well, I don't know about one hundred dollars," Marquis says. "How about fifty?" I look at Marquis like he's lost his mind.

"Okay, that will definitely help. Thanks Marquis. You too, Jazz?" Jasmine looks at me and smiles.

"Are you crazy? What are you talking about? And Marquis are you crazy too? Jasmine, why should I give you *any* money? I'm not rich. I mean, *I* should be getting free books, free lunch and anything else they are giving away for free. If I gave anybody any money, it would be Mom or Jackson or even you if you really needed it. Why would I give fifty dollars for free books? Why can't they just go to the library? They can check out tons of books, for free! Do you know how long it takes me to earn fifty dollars? Five weeks of chores and I get fifty-five dollars. You want me to work for five weeks so some kids can have free books? Marquis, you just saved four hundred dollars. You keep going along with Jasmine and you're going to be broke. No. I'm too poor to give away any money. So get out of my room." I get up and show Jasmine the door. Marquis looks shocked like I said something wrong.

Jasmine stays seated on my desk, like I'm not the boss of her. She says, "You know Jazz, I used to think the same way. You save all your money for yourself. I used to spend all my money on myself for concert tickets, clothes, music and all the stuff I saw on TV. After my bad experience with Quick Check Cashers and that stupid loan, I realized that it's not worth it. I also realize that even though I never feel like I have enough, I'm blessed to have more than most people. And Jazz, you see all these books in this room? Granddad *gave* them to you. They were *free* to you. He probably spent hundreds of dollars buying us books and he worked harder for his money than you do. So, just think about it...because not everyone has a granddad." She gets up and walks out my door.

CHAPTER 31

I'M STRETCHED

Jazz Ellington
May 15

    Granddad, I really wish you were here. I feel like a rubber band, stretched between Jackson and Jasmine. Jackson's car got repossessed. It was scary. I thought we were being attacked by a bear! Long story. But even after the scary part, it's embarrassing. Everybody in the neighborhood knows about it. At first Jackson was mad. Now he walks around like it didn't happen. He keeps getting calls from collectors chasing him to pay back his car loan, but he says, "Why should I pay? You got the car?" Mom says now his credit report is as bad as hers, but it took her six years to mess up her credit. It took him less than six months! And Jasmine is another story. She wants me to give her one hundred dollars so she can give away books to kids. Can you believe it? I don't recall you ever telling me to give money away. Maybe the kids should save their money like you taught me. I've been saving since I was five and now I have over two thousand dollars. Key has been saving for one year and he already has over four hundred dollars. Instead of a book, I think these kids need a savings plan...so they can buy their own books!

CHAPTER 32

MY RENEWAL

I walk into the bank branch after school a few days later and find my Miss Benjamin on the phone at her desk. She waves for me to come have a seat.

"Well hello, Mister Ellington," she says as she hangs up. I like the sound of Mister Ellington. "I haven't seen you in months and I think you've grown a few inches. How can I help you today?"

"I got this letter in the mail. It says it's a renewal notice for my certificate of deposit." I hand Miss Benjamin the letter.

"Yes. It has been almost one year since you opened your two thousand dollar certificate of deposit...your CD. You have earned sixty dollars in interest over the past year at the three- percent interest rate because you agreed to keep your money in the bank for a one-year term. Now that the term is ending, we send a renewal notice. The notice says that you can automatically renew the CD.

That means that you can agree to keep your money in the bank for another one-year term. Or you can move the money to a savings account or another CD for a different term."

"Why would I move the money?" I ask.

"Well different CD terms offer different rates," Miss Benjamin continues. "Let's see. Our current rate for one year is three-and-a-half percent. So you could earn a little more if you renew, but we also have other CD terms and interest rates. You may want to come back with your mother so that we can discuss all your options." Miss Benjamin hands me back my renewal notice, but she looks at me like she can tell something is wrong. "Is there anything else I can help you with?"

I hesitate then say, "When Marquis asked you to sponsor the Raiders by giving our football team a donation last year, you said no. I told Marquis that banks don't *give away* money. You *make* money by providing loans to people to buy homes and cars. I mean why would you give away money?"

"Well Jazz, the bank *does* give away money...I mean donate to organizations. We have a team here at the Bank that chooses the organizations. And this year the team decided to donate to home-less shelters so that more people have a warm place to sleep and food to eat. Unfortunately, we can't donate to every organization. I'm sorry we couldn't give to the Raiders this year." Miss Benjamin looks sorry too.

"Well the bank makes a lot of money. You can afford to give away money. My sister wants me to give her one hundred dollars for the Yancey Book Fair. She must think I'm rich." I say.

"Well, you don't have to be rich to give. I mean some people give because they have more money than others and they feel guilty. Do you feel a little guilty because you have more money in the bank than others?"

"Yeah, a little," I say as I look down on the ground. First time I admitted that.

"Well, my understanding from your mother is that you work hard for your allowance. It's also not easy to save. So you shouldn't feel guilty." She continues, "Some people give to organizations or causes that they truly care about. Their heart or faith leads them to give because they want to help. Do you care about the kids who go to the Yancey Book Fair?"

"Yeah," I say. "Most of the kids in my class say they went last year. Some of them are my friends. It's just that, they can get books from the library."

"Yes, that's true. But someone has to bring them to the library and take them to bring the books back. Also, borrowing something, even from the library, is not the same as having your own." Miss Benjamin bends her head to look me in the eye and says, "Maybe think about what your granddad would do." Whoa. I didn't expect her to say that. I nod, get up and leave the bank.

CHAPTER 33

LEARNING THE 4 P'S

Only two more weeks before school is out and it's a heat wave. Everybody on the bus, including me, is trying to get close to the windows. Marquis is eating a cup of ice he got from the coach to cool his body down and is talking between crunches.

"Man, I can't believe you aced that history pop quiz. I mean I would have done better had I known there was going to be a quiz," Marquis says. "At least we don't have to study this weekend. Are you coming with me to the new Scrub-Away tomorrow to count cars?"

At the last Kitchen Cabinet meeting, me and Marquis agreed to check out the new Scrub-Away that opened last week. Marquis' mom and dad decided not to hand over the keys to Grandma's Hand Car Wash to Scrub-Away. They decided to compete for business. Mister Hill told us about a business article he read that said businesses compete with the four "P's"...*product, price, promotion* and *place*. He said that by Scrub-Away invading our neighborhood, they were going to have an equal *place* to Grandma's Hand Car Wash. But their *product*—a machine car wash instead of a hand car wash—is not as good. Jackson and his team take better care of the cars and are nicer to customers. He said that *promotion* was advertising and that Grandma's Hand Car Wash or Scrub-Away didn't have any commercials. So the only thing Grandma's had to fix was *price*. At twenty dollars per wash, we could not compete with Scrub-Away's ten dollars. So we reduced our price to fifteen dollars a wash. We also now offer a Car Wash Plan of five washes for sixty dollars or twelve dollars a wash. The price change decreases profit—so it will take longer to pay back the bank loan. But Mister and Mrs. Hill believe we can still be successful. Now Marquis and I are going to see how successful Scrub-Away is.

"Sure, I'll meet you there," I say. "Right after I stop by the bookstore."

CHAPTER 34

MY LESSON

Finally the last week of school! It's a short week with school ending in two days. I feel great. I walk into the community center carrying a big box and look for Jasmine. The center looks different with all the decorations. And the sun shines so bright that it's hard to see.

"Hey Jazz," Jasmine yells out as she waves me over to a group of tables. I can tell she's surprised to see me. I'm not surprised to see her surrounded by her group of friends. But they don't look so weird this time. They're all busy unpacking boxes of books and setting up for the Fair.

"What's in the box?" Jasmine asks me. Everybody stops working and looks at me.

"Well, I guess my donation. The store put them in a box because a shopping bag was too small," I say. I feel nervous and excited, but try to act cool.

Jasmine takes the box from me, sets it on a table and opens it. "Wow!" everybody says at the same time like a choir. Then, to my surprise, they start jumping up and down, clapping, laughing and running over to try to hug me. I duck and laugh too. Jasmine slowly takes out the books. She looks at some of the titles like *Save Money Today* and *How to Make Money* and *How Do Banks Work?* Then she starts crying. Not again! But this time it feels different.

She says, "I can see that you spent more than the one hundred dollars I asked for. And that you're giving more than books. You're giving a part of you and our granddad. All these books teach kids about money. And they show the importance of saving. You're sharing Granddad's lessons to our family."

I go over to my big sister and do something I rarely do. I let her hug me. And I say, "Granddad always *told* us, 'To be successful, you got to have bank.' But what he *showed* us was how much he loved teaching kids about money. What I learned about money all comes from Granddad. I've been going crazy all year trying to understand why nobody listened to Granddad. Then I realize that I may not be able to convince grown-ups. I just turned eleven! But maybe I can help kids—like Granddad helped us. I hope these books will help."

Then I remember how much I hate hugs and squirm away and say, "Now let's get these books ready. Kids will be here any minute." We all laugh and start setting them up.

CHAPTER 35

ALWAYS

Jazz Ellington
June 23

Granddad, I finally got it. Yes, I got bank! But you taught me so much more. Now I know it's all about how I use my money and not letting it use me–by buying stuff I really don't need. I could use it to buy a house one day or pay for college or start a business or donate to an organization. Money has a purpose. I'm not sure what that purpose is for me. I'm still trying to figure that out. But even if I get it wrong–like Jackson did when he bought a new car he couldn't afford or Jasmine did when she took out that allowance loan from Quick Check Cashers–I'll just keep trying until I get it right. I'll learn from my mistakes and start saving all over again.

I miss you a lot and wish you were still here. Your lessons will be with me always.

Love, Jazz

My Glossary

How I Describe Old School Banking Terms

Account balance The amount of money in your bank account.

Allowance Money given to kids who do chores on a regular basis. Ask your mom or dad for an allowance, so you can save like me.

Automatic deposit Money that is regularly deposited in one bank account from another bank account or a pay check by computers. A good way to save money.

Bank A company that keeps your money safe, helps your money grow and can provide a loan if you qualify. Banks try to "recycle" deposit dollars back into the communities they serve by making loans. A bank provides other banking services too.

Bank account A way to keep money in a bank, like a savings account or a checking account. Ask your mom or dad to open a bank account for you.

Bounced check If you give a store a check to pay for something and you don't have enough money in your checking account, the bank sends the check right back unpaid. The check bounces back and you get a ChexSystems record. Don't bounce checks.

Budget A plan for spending and saving money to make sure you don't spend more than you have. You list income and expenses in your budget.

Certificate of deposit or CD A bank account that pays the same interest rate for a fixed amount of time—like six months or one year—if you agree to keep your money in the bank for that time. Banks are willing to pay a higher interest rate for a longer amount of time (like 6 months, 1 year or 3 years), which they call a term.

Check Cashers	Companies that cash checks and charge high fees. They also offer payday loans with high interest rates.
Checking account	A bank account that is used for writing checks that are paid immediately, or on demand.
Checks	Written orders telling a bank to give a certain amount of money to the person or business named on the check. You need to make sure you have enough money in your account to pay for the check! See the Bounced check entry.
ChexSystems	A company that tells every bank if you had problems with your bank accounts, like a lot of bounced checks. If you have a ChexSystems record, you may not be able to open a new bank account.
Collateral	Something of value, like a bank account, car or a house, that can be used to guarantee that you will repay a loan. If you take out a loan with collateral and you don't pay the loan back, the bank can take the collateral and sell it to get its money back. So, a bank is more willing to give you a loan if you have collateral.
Credit agency	A company that keeps track of who you owe, how much you owe and whether you pay back your loans on time. And they give you a credit score.
Credit score	A number that tells banks whether you pay back your loans on time. If you have a high credit score, banks are more likely to give you a new loan. If you have a low credit score, banks may not give you a loan or they may require collateral.
Deposit	Money put into a bank account.
Donate	To give money or other things of value to support an organization that does good work for your community. It's nice to donate.
Federal Deposit Insurance Corporation or FDIC	A government agency that makes sure banks follow the rules and that people don't lose money in their bank accounts.

I Got Bank!

Foreclosure	If you do not pay back your mortgage or home loan, a bank can throw you out and sell it to someone else to get its money back. You may still owe the bank more money. Foreclosure is bad for your credit score.
Interest	It's extra money. If you have a savings account, you have your savings plus extra money that the bank gives you for saving. If you take out a loan, you pay back the loan plus extra money. Your mom or dad will pay interest to the bank for lending them money.
Loan	Money given to some one that must be paid back over time, usually with interest.
Money laundering	When somebody takes money from crimes like selling drugs and deposits it in a bank to try to make it look like "clean cash" that came from a real business. Also, when somebody puts small amounts of money in the bank several times (under $10,000) to avoid paying taxes. Don't launder money. People go to jail for this.
Mortgage	A loan that uses a home or other real estate property as collateral. Also called a home loan.
Payday loan	A loan you can get from a check casher that you have to pay back when you get paid. The interest rate is very high.
Profit	Money that businesses have left over from their sales after their expenses have been paid.
Repossession	If you don't pay back your car loan, a bank will send the repo man to take back your car and sell it to some one else to get its money back. You may still owe the bank more money. Repossession is bad for your credit score.
Saving account	A bank account that pays interest on what you save. Ask your mom or dad to open a savings account for you.
Statement	A list of all the money events that happen in a bank account over a period of time—usually a month or a quarter (3 months). Your bank will send you a bank statement that includes your account balance.

86

Taxes
Money that you have to pay to the government from your pay check or from your business profit so we can have free schools, an army, libraries and other services.

Withdrawal
Money taken out of a bank account. Try not to withdraw too much so that you can save more money.

ABOUT THE AUTHOR

TERI WILLIAMS has committed her life to increasing financial literacy and financial services to urban communities. She grew up in "the projects" of Bridgeport, Connecticut and also lived in the rural town of Indiantown, Florida.

Through hard work and the support of many people, she earned a B.A. with distinction from Brown University and an M.B.A. with honors from Harvard University. She has worked in financial services for over 30 years. Teri Williams is president and on the board of directors of OneUnited Bank—one of the largest black-owned banks in the country.

She has received numerous notations and awards for her contribution to urban communities from the Urban League, the NAACP, and the National Black MBA Association. She lives in Chestnut Hill, Massachusetts. Williams is married to Kevin Cohee, and they have two children, Erin and Kevin Cohee Jr.

88